K. Srinivasa Raghavan

The Date of the Maha Bharata War

and the Kali Yugadhi

K. Srinivasa Raghavan

The Date of the Maha Bharata War
and the Kali Yugadhi

ISBN/EAN: 9783337378165

Printed in Europe, USA, Canada, Australia, Japan

Cover: Foto ©Andreas Hilbeck / pixelio.de

More available books at **www.hansebooks.com**

The Date of the Maha Bharata War
and
The Kali Yugadhi

Prof. K. Srinivasa Raghavan,
B.A. (Hons.) Math., Dip. in Geog., Dip. in P.Ed.

SRINIVASANAGAR, TAMBARAM
SAKA 1891

PREFACE

With the name of the Lord of Kurukshetra on my lips and my head at his feet, I humbly present this to the earnest reader.

Sriman Vidwan Melma Narasimha Thathacharya Swamigal and Prof. R. S. Chakravarthy, M.A. advised me and guided me in the presentation of the subject matter. Sri. N. Subba Narayanan, B.A. has kindly borne the entire cost of the publication of this book. I must thank them for their affection and their unstinted help.

I must thank the press for their kind co-operation.

Saka 1891, Sowmya
Sarad Ruthu, 1st Isa month
Badra Sukla Dwadasi } Prof. K. SRINIVASARAGHAVAN
Sravishta Nakshatra
Tuesday, 23 Sep. 1969

Determination of
THE DATE OF THE MAHA BHARATA WAR

INTRODUCTION

I have gone carefully through all the essays of the occidental and oriental scholars in determining the date of the Maha Bharata War. Those scholars have variously fixed the date ranging from 1919 B.C. to 315 B.C. Most of their ideas are empirical and not a few of them are the product of fanciful imagination or pre-conceived notions. It is now possible dispassionately to determine the correct date with a high degree of accuracy, and this is based on astronomical data and the internal evidence of the Maha Bharata alone. We may in fact justly and properly style the date of the Maha Bharata war, which the science of astronomy has now in controvertibly fixed on 22 Nov. 3067 B.C., as the true anchor sheet of Indian chronology and history, as every date indicated by Indian astronomy and supported by Ancient Indian Puranic history depends on it.

1. In fixing the date of the Maha Bharata war, the first step is to determine the date of birth of Sri Krishna, as his horoseope is well known.

2. Since Maha Rishi Veda Vyasa gives the positions of the Sun, Moon, Rahu, Saturn, Jupiter, Mars and Venus at the time of the Maha Bharata war, also the positions of the Sun and Moon and the winter solstice at the time of Bheeshma's death, a few days after the M. B. war, the exact date of the beginning of the M. B. war is next determined.

3. Sri Krishna left the world 35 years after the M. B. war. Since the positions of the sun and moon at that time are known, the date of his death is fixed.

4. Rajasuya was performed 15 years before the M. B. war, and the positions of the Sun and Moon on that day are given. Therefore the date of the Rajasuya is fixed. The Yudhishtira Era began the next day on Margasira Sukla Prathama. Therefore its date is fixed.

5. In the course of the paper it is proposed to show that all the astronomical data given by Sri Veda Vyasa are completely consistent.

6. During the days of the Maha Bharata war, the Vedanga Jyotisha alone was in vogue. The Zodiac was divided by the nakshatra segments, and Sravishta was the first Nakshatra. The months were luni solar. Five sidereal years consituted a yuga of 62 lunations. The Yuga began with the Sun and Moon at Sravishta i.e Magha Sukla Prathama. One month was added at the end of the third year and another at the end of the fifth year of the Yuga. The tropical year was divided into six Ruthus = Twelve solar months. The twelve months beginning with Sarad Ruthu were Isa, Urja, Sahas, Sahasya, Tapas, Tapasya, Madhu, Madhava, Sucra, Suchi, Nabhas, Nabhasya. The presiding dieties of the months are Kesava, Narayana, Madhava, Govinda, Vishnu, Madhusudana, Trivikrama, Vamana, Sridhara, Hrishikesa, Padmanabha, and Damodara. The first month began with the Sarad Ruthu i.e Autumnal Equinox, which was therefore the beginning of the year. During Sri Krishna's time, Margasira was the first month of the year, and the year began with the Durga Puja and Sarada Navarathri at the beginning of the Sarad Ruthu. The twelve Rasis and the related twelve months were then unknown.

They were introduced into the Hindu Astronomy by the Siddhanta Astronomers of the A. D. years. Apparently they got it from the Yavanas of Western Asia.

7. The present standard Zodiac of the Govt. of India was fixed in 1956 A. D. Spica or Chitra Nakshatra is at the 180º th degree of this Zodiac. This is different from the Zodiac of the Vedanga Jyotisha. The difference is 1° 46' i.e to obtain the longitude on the Vedanga Jyotisha Zodiac, 1° 46' should be added to the longitude of the zodiac of the Govt. of India.

Moreover the Vedic Rishis used only Polar longitudes, and not the celestial longitude, which is given nowadays in all the Indian Panchangs (Almanacs), and this is evidently not the correct one to determine the positions of the planets.

8. The metod adopted by me to determine the longitude of the planets on any given date, is a slightly modified and improved one of that given by Sri L. Narayana Rao in his Perpetual Ephemeris. A similar method is given by Dewan Bahadur Swami Kannu Pillai in his "Indian Ephemeris". This is also used for verifying the results. The longitudes given are the visible longitudes at Kurukshetra, and not the mean longitudes. The time of day is from sunrise at Kurukshetra (or Ujjain).

CHAPTER I

The Date of birth of Sri Krishna

According to accepted tradition, Sri Krishna was born in the Bhadrapada month, Krishna Ashtami, Rohini Nakshatra, at about midnight, when five planets were in exaltation and the other two in their own houses.

The chart of the horoscope is as follows :—

		L	
	Rahu	Moon	
			Jup
	Rasi		
Mars			Sun
		Venus Sat	Mer

European scholars who could not imagine of the hoary tradition of Bharat, searched for this combination of planetary positions from 1000 B.C. to 500 A.D. When they found that they could not fix the date, the only other alternative for them was to say that Sri Krishna is a mythical person, and the puranas false stories. Poor scholars! They should have searched for his date of birth near the beginning of the Kali Yuga Era i.e about 3100 B.C. Then they would have found out that he was born at 11.40 P.M. on Friday 27th July 3112 B.C., when the planets were disposed as follows :—

   (i) Lagna and Moon 52° 15' Rohini (4)

  (ii) Jupiter 91° 16' Punarvasu (4)

 (iii) Sun 148° 15' uthara Phalguni (1)

 (iv) Mercury 172° 33' Hasta (4)

  (v) Venus 180° 15' Chitra (3)

 (vi) Saturn 209° 57' Visakha (3)

 (vii) Mars 270° 1' uthara Ashada (2)

(viii) Rahu 16° 1' Bharani (1)

A close look at the positions of the planets reveals that Jupiter, Venus, and Mars just rushed into their positions for the sake of Lord Krishna, while the Moon, Sun, Mercury and Saturn lingered a little longer to be there at the time of the birth of the Lord Most wonderful! Rahu in the 12th. place made him an invincible warrior.

For fixing the position of the planets, the method adopted is that given by Sri L. Narayana Rao M.A. in his " Perpetual Ephemeris ", and by Dewan Bahadur Swami Kannu Pillai in his Indian Ephemeins. But I have slightly improved the technique, and I use the sidereal periods of the planets as accepted by modern astronomers.

(i) Sun and Moon.

On Saturday, 10th Jan. 3104 B.C, at 5 P.M. the sun and the moon were together at 312.61.

    92 lunations = 2716.814 days

    7 Sidereal years = 2556.798

Difference = 160.016 days = 157°. 826 of the Zodiac. i.e New Moon occurred 7 years 160.016 days before 5 P.M. on 10th Jan. 3104 B.C., and at New Moon the sun and Moon were at 312°.61 − 157°.826 = 154°78.

Therefore the previous Krishna Sapthami ended at

(a) 154.78 − 7.74 = 147.04
or (b) 154.78 − 8.10 = 146.68 } Range

ie (a) 2716.814 + 7.872 = 2724.686 days
or (b) 2716.814 + 8.21 = 2725.024 days } Range

before 5 P.M. on 10th Jan. 3104 B. C.

The corresponding Julian Day reckoned from sunrise at Kurukshetra is

(a) 587691.46 − 2724.686 = 584972.774 days
or (b) 587691.46 − 2725.024 = 584972.436 days } Range

The position of the Moon at that time was

(a) 147.04 − 96 = 51.05
(b) 146.68 − 96 = 50.68 } Range — Last quarter of Rohini.

Converting to the Zodiac of Vedanga Jyotisha, by adding 1° 15', the sun was at 148° 15' and the Moon at 52° 15'.

Hence it was just at 11.40 P.M. on Friday, 584973rd Julian day, Bhadrapada month, Krishna Ashtami, Rohini Nakshatra, Lord Krishna was born, with the *sun at 148° 15'* and the *Moon at 52° 15'*. The corresponding date is Friday, 27th July 3112 B. C.

(ii) Position of Rahu = 230° 22' + 144° 24' + 1° 15'
= 376° 01' = *16° 01'*

(iii) Saturn :

170 cycles of saturn = 1829067.37 days
5008 cycles of sun = 1829206.55 days
∴ Saturn is ahead of sun by 4° 39'.
The corresponding Kali Day is 1829206.55 − 3493
= 1825713.55 = 11 Sep 1897 A. D.
∴ Position of Saturn = 213°21' − 4° 39' + 1° 15' = *209°57'*

(iv) Jupiter :

412 cycles of Jupiter = 1815353.0396 days

4970 cycles of sun   = 1815326.74 days

∴ Jupiter is behind sun by 2° 15'. The corresponding Kali Day = 1815326.74 − 3493 = 1811833.74 = 11 Sep 1859 A. D

∴ Position of Jupiter = 87° 46' + 2° 15' + 1° 15' = *91° 16'*

(v) Mars :

2643 cycles of Mars = 1815687.2017 days

4971 cycles of Sun = 1815691.5528 days

∴ Mars is ahead of sun by 2° 16'. The corresponding Kali Day = 1812198.5528 = 10th Sep 1860 A. D.

∴ Position of Mars = 271° 02' − 2°16' + 1°15' = *270°01'*

(vi) Venus :

8074 cycles of Venus = 1814242.219 days

4969 cycles of sun   = 1814230.5256 days

∵ Venus is behind the sun by 18° 45'. The corresponding Kali Day = 1810738 = 10 Sep 1856 A. D.

∴ Position of Venus = 160°15' + 18°45' + 1°15' = *180°15'*

(vii) Mercury :

20628 cycles of Mercury = 1814595.8587 days

4968 cycles of sun   = 1814596.2713 days

∴ Mercury is a head of sun by 1° 35'.

The corresponding Kali Day = 1811103.27 = 11 Sep 1857 A. D.

∴ Position of Mercury = 172°23' − 1°35' + 1°15' = *172° 33'*

Note : The positions obtained by referring to Swami Kannu Pillai's "Indian Ephemeris" are as follows :—(i) Saturn 208° 59'. (ii) Jupiter 90°23' (iii) Mars 271° 36' (iv) Venus 180° 14' (v) Mercury 171° 04'

The two results are practically the same.

CHAPTER II
Determination of the birth days of the Pandavas

(from the astronomical data supplied by Maha
Rishi Veda Vyasa in the Adi Parvan of the
Maha Bharata.)

(i) Yudhishtira was born on Sukla Panchami, Jyeshta
Nakshatra Day in the Abijit Muhurta—(8th Muhurta of the
day; 1 Muhurta = 48 minutes): Adi Parvan—7 Sambava
Parva—ch 129—sl 21.

(ii) Almost a year later Bheemasena was born on
Krishna Trayodasi, Magha Nakshatra Day, in the Pitiryam
or Rohini Muhurta (9th of the day). chap. 130—sl. 66.

(iii) Arjuna was born on the day with Poorva and
uthara Phalguni Nakshtras. His fourteenth birthday was
on the first day of the month of Madhava, Sri Krishna was
born in the third month after Arjuna—Ch. 132—17 and
Ch. 134—9.

(iv) Ch. 133—24:—The children were born at one per
year, like the 5 years of a Yuga.

(v) Ch. 134—9:—Krishna was junior to Bala Rama by
one year and 3 months.

(vi) These data, together with the date of birth of
Sri Krishna, fix the birth days of the three Pandavas. Let
us consider Arjuna first. Since Sri Krishna was born in the
month of *Suchi*, he was born in the month of Madhava
[months in order are—Madhu, *Madhava*, Sucra, Suchi,
Nabhas, Nabhasya,...]. On the new moon day following
Sri Krishna's birth the sun was at 154.8. Two lunations
before, the new moon was with the sun at 96.8. $3\frac{3}{4}$ days

later the sun was at 100.6, and the moon at 146.8 i.e Sukla Chathurthi, Uthara Phalguni Nakshatra. The corresponding Julian Day is 584927, Monday. This is again verified by the next statement regarding the 14th Birth day.

13 years later the corresponding New Moon was with the sun at 96.5 − 22.0 = 74.5.

3¾ days later the sun was at 78.3.

Note: The month of Madhu was from 48° to 78° and the month of Madhava was from 79 to 109 etc. Hence it is seen that the 14th birth day of Arjuna fell on the first day of the month of Madhava!!

(vii) 24 lunations before Sri Krishna's birth, i.e 708.9 days before, the new moon was with the sun at 176.1. 4.5 days later, the sun was at 180.6, and the moon at 236.1 i.e Sukla Panchami, Jyeshta Nakshatra.

This is the birth day of Yudhishtira, Julian Day, 584277, Tuesday [3114 B.C.].

(viii) 12 lunations or 354.43 days after Yudhishtira's birth, the New Moon was with the sun at 165.4. Three days before the sun was at 162.4, and the Moon was at 125.4 i.e Krishna Trayodasi, Magha Nakshatra. This is the birth day of Bheemasena, Julian Day 584624, Saturday [3113 B.C.].

(ix) Bala Rama was younger then Yudhishtira and older than Bheemasena. The sun was at Rohini (47°) at his birth. There fore he was 229 days younger than Yudhishtira—Julian Day 584506, Sunday.

2

Birth days of the Pandavas and Sri Krishna

Name	Position of Sun	Position of Moon	Thithi	Muhurta	Difference in days	Birth date Julian day	Remarks
Yudhishtira	181° Chitra	236° Jyeshta	Sukla Panchami	Abijit 8th—Day	0	31 Aug. 3114 B. C. 584277 Tuesday	
Bala Rama	47 Rohini	—	—	—	229	584506 Sunday	
Bheemassena	162 Hasta	125 Magha	Krishna Trayodasi	Pitir yam 9th—Day	347	584624 Saturday	
Arjuna	101 Pushya	147 uthara Phalguni	Sukla Chathurthi	—	650	584927 Monday	
Sri Krishna	147 uthara Phalguni	52 Rohini	Krishna Ashtami	Abijit 8th—Night	696	584973 Friday 27 July 3112 B. C.	Wonderful Horoscope

CHAPTER III
Bheeshma's death

1. Udhishtira celebrated the Raja Suya on the Amavasya day with Jyeshta and Moola Nakshatras. Hence 15 years later at the time of the Mahabharata War, the Amavasya was at the beginning of Jyeshta ie with the sun at 224.75.

2. In the Udyoga Parva ch 142, Sri Krishna tells Karna, just before leaving Hastinapura, that Amavasya comes on Jyeshta Day. Hence this Amavasya was with the sun at $224.^\circ 75$.

3. Santi Parva ch. 46, Anusasani Parva ch. 272-274. It is stated that Bheeshma died at Midday on Magha Sukla Ashtami, Rohini Nakshatra. Therefore the position of the sun on that day was $224^\circ.75 + 87^\circ 3$ (3 lunations) $+ 6^\circ.80$ Ashtami $= 318^\circ.85$.

4. Again it is stated that Bheeshma died as soon as the sun's chariot turned north. Therefore utharayana or winter solstice was with the sun at 317°.

5. It is also stated that Bheeshma died on Sukla Ashtami Day i.e when the Moon was 90° from the sun i.e at 49°. This is in complete agreement with the statement that it was Rohini Nakshatra.

6. Because winter solstice was with the sun at 317°, the Vernal Equinox was with the sun at 47°.

7. By the law of the precession of the equinoxes, it is well known that in 3100 B.C., the Vernal Equinox (r) was at 47°. The time of Bheeshma's death and the Maha Bharata War was about 3100 B.C.

CHAPTER IV
Date of the Mahabharata War

Introduction

The date of the Mahabharata is quite important to Indian History. The whole of Indian History entirely depends upon the date of the Maha Bharata war, for the dates of accassion of kings of the various Hindu dynasties are invariably calculated in all our Puranas and other works of authoritry from the time of Mahabharata War.

—T. S. Narayana Sastri, B.A.B.L

If we wish to adopt the three fold chronological classification of history in relation to the progress of civilisation and of human events in India also, the date of the Mahabharata war acquires a characteristic importance. A comprehensive view of Indian civilisation as unfolded by Indian Literature shows distinctly that what may be called the Ancient History of India was really at an end by the time of this war which was thus chronologically coincident with the commencement of the Mediaeval History of India.

—Prof. M. Rangacharya, M.A.

Section. 1. Let us now consider the references to the Maha Bharata War, the Yudhishtira Era, Kali Era, and Saptha Rishi Era.

(i) Varaha Mihira—Brihat Samhita XIII-3. The sages (Saptha Rishis) were in Magha in Yudhishtira's time.

(ii) Vriddha Garga quoted by Bhattotpala—At the Junction of Dwapara and Kali, the Saptha Rishis were in Magha.

(iii) Vishnu, Bagavata etc. Puranas state that Kali Yuga began in the 75th year of Magha.

(iv) When 35 years were over after the Mahabharata War at the time indicated by the curse of Gandhari, the Yadavas saw bad omens portending their destruction—Mousala Parva.

(v) Yudhishtira ruled for 36 years after the Maha Bharata War and then left the world — Mahabharata, Swarga Rohana Parva.

(vi) The Yudhishtira Era was started 25 years after Kali Era i.e with the beginning of the Poorva Phalguni cycle of the Saptha Rishi Era—Sri V. Thiru Venkatacharya–Popular Astronomy.

(vii) The Inscription in the temple of Hanuman at Jaisalmer, Rajaputana states that the Commencement of Yudhishtira Era was from the coronation of Yudhishtira at Indraprasta.

(viii) Maha Bharata Adi Parva—7 Sambava Parva, ch76 (Kumbakonam Edition) and ch 137 [Calcutta Edition]—"Vyasa told his mother 2 months after Pandu's death, that—"Dharma is dying and Adharma is getting powerful." He then took her away from Hastinapura."

(ix) Vana Parva chap 151. Hanuman Says "Kali Yuga has already come."

(x) Salya Parva—ch. 61—Krishna states that the unfair fight was due to Kali's influence.

(xi) Udyoga Parva—ch 142-Krishna during his conversation with Karna stated repeatedly that Kali Yuga had come.

(xii) Mousala Parva—ch.1.

" Though Kali has come, it was like Krita Yuga because of Sri Krishna "

(xiii) Mousala Parva—ch. 3

Sahadeva tells Udhishtira that "Kali has come because of the departure of Sri Krishna." Immediately they prepare for Maha Prasthana.

(xiv) Arya Bhatiya—Gitika 5.

Kali began from the Maha Prasthana of the Pandavas.

(xv) Vishnu, Bagavata and other Puranas—

Kali Yuga began on the day Sri Krishna left the world.

(xvi) Bagavata Purana—

Udhishtira states that "even after seven months Arjuna has not returned from Dwaraka." Then his preparation for Maha Prasthana on Arjuna's return, shows that it was 7 months after the Yadava slaughter, Yudhishtira gave up his kingdom, and went away after crowning Parikshit.

More over it is usual for Vanaprasthas and Sanyasins to move out after the rainy season. Dridharashtra left Hastinapura for the forest in the month of Margasira, and so did Udhishtira— on the Vijaya Dasami Day.

Hence the conclusion is that Kali Yuga began during the life time of Sri Krishna, and it was there at the time of the Maha Bharata War. But reckoning started after the Pandavas left on Maha Prasthana, and Parikshit began to rule, i.e. exactly 36 years after the beginning of the Maha Bharatha War.

Section 2.

The Maha Bharata is teeming with plenty of astronomical information regarding its own age. It is proposed to arrange them in order and determine the exact date of the Maha Bharata war. This paper is based entirely on the many Astronomical data supplied by Sri Veda Vyasa, which are all consistent.

(A) The following statements are seen in the Maha Bharata—Udyoga Parvan :—

(i) Sri Krishna left Upaplaviya for Hastinapura on the mission of peace in the Maithra Muhurta (3rd muhurta of the morning from 7.36 A.M. to 8.24 A.M.) on Sukla Dwadasi, Revati Day, in the month of Krithika. En route he halted for a day at a town called Vrikasthala—Chap. 82, 83, 85.

(ii) He reached Hastinapura on Bharani Day ch. 89.

(iii) He met various persons to discuss the conditions for averting a War. The meetings went on up to Pushya day—ch. 90 and 91.

(iv) On Pushya Day (Krishna Panchami), Duryodana finally refused all conditions for peace, and ordered his men to prepare the battlefield of Kurukshetra—ch. 180.

(v) Sri Krishna left Hastinapura on Uthara Phalguni Day with Karna in his chariot. Their conversation is very interesting and illuminating. Sri Krishna told Karna that the seventh day from then, Jyeshta Day, was Amavasya, and asked him to advise Duryodana to begin the war preparations on that Day—ch. 142.

(vi) He returns to Upaplaviya on Chitra day. Three days later i.e on Anuradha Day, Sri Bala Rama comes to Upaplaviya to know the result of Sri Krishna's mission, and coming to know of its failure, he decides to go on a pilgrimage, and leaves the place for Dwaraka with Pradyumna and others—ch. 157.

(vii) On the following Pushya Day, Sri Krishna with the Pandavas moved towards Kurukshetra (stated twice in the Salya Parva—ch. 35).

(viii) 17 days after his return from Upaplaviya, on Punarvasu day, Balarama started on his pilgrimage from Prabhasa, at the mouth of the River Saraswathy—Salya Parva ch. 34. A number of chapters following ch. 34, discribe the pilgrimage of Bala Rama along the course of the River Saraswathy, dotted with many holy Rishi Ashramas. 42 days after starting on his pilgrimage i.e on Sravana Day, he comes to Kurukshetra, on the evening of the 18th Day of the Maha Bharata War. The 19th morning, when Duryodana died was Krishna Paksha Chathurdasi, Sravana Nakshatra i.e 59th day from the Jyeshta Amavasya.

(ix) 2 days after Bala Rama left Upaplaviya i.e on Moola day, Rukmi, the great warrior and brother of Rukmini came to the Pandava camp and offered his help. It was refused and he went away—Udyoga Parva chap. 158.

This disproves the conjecture of many scholars who state that the Maha Bharata war began on Jyeshta Amavasya day.

(B)

(i) Udyoga Parva ch. 142 and 143 give the following information (astronomical).

    (a) The day was Uthara Phalguni day, when Sri Krishna left Hastinapura after the failure of his peace mission.

(b) Seven days later, it was Jyeshta Amavasya day.

(c) Saturn was *very bright* and was with *Rohini Nakshatra.*

(d) Rahu was approaching the sun

(e) The moon was approaching the Amavasya.

(ii) Bheeshma Parva—A number of astronomical observations are given here. They are considered seperately in an appendix.

(iii) Mousala Parva chap. 3 :—

" When Amavasya came on the 13th day, Sri Krishna said," Again Rahu has caused Poornima on Chathurdasi day. Such a thing happened at the approach of the Maha Bharata War. It has now come for our destruction .. "He then found it was the 36th year after the Maha Bharata War, and was reminded of the curse of Gandhari."

(iv) Sri Vaishnava Guruparampara and " Eedu " Commentary of Nammalwar's Thiruvoimozhi—"Sri Krishna left the world in the beginning of Kali Yuga on Friday, Chaitra Sukla, Prathama, Utharaproshtapada Nakshatra, and Sri Satagopa was born 43 days later in the month of Vaisakha, on Friday, Sukla Chathurdasi day, Poornima Thithi and Visakha Nakshatra.

(C) The might battle of Drona on the 14th night is very graphically described by Maha Rishi Veda Vyasa [Drona Parva ch. 185—188]. At about midnight Gatothkacha was killed by Karna. The fury of the battle was tremendous, but the warriors on both sides were very tired. Just then, at about 1 A.M. Arjuna declared a short truce for one muhurta (48 minutes), *till moonrise.* The moon rose at about 2 A.M. "when ⅓ of the night was still left". The description of the moonrise is excellent, and the battle that followed it was terrible. Drona became mad with fury and killed Virata and

3

Drupada at about 5 A.M. The sun rose on the 15th morning
to give a short respite for both parties for Sandyopasana.
Therefore it was Krishna Paksha Dasami on the 15 morning,
and hence it was Krishna Chathurdasi on the 19th morning.

(D) On Jyeshta Day both sides went to Kurukshetra
which was still wet and slushy. The Pandavas chose the
western side on the bank of the Hiranya Nadi, while
Duryodana chose the eastern side (Udyoga Parva). They
started cutting canals, building comfortable camps, houses
and palaces, laid beautiful roads, etc. Duryodana's camp
was like another Hastinapura, connecting it by well laid
chariot roads. The camps were well provided with plenty of
good water, food, medicines and armoury. There were
plenty of doctors, nurses, attendants etc. All this took just
only one month. The next amavasya (30 days after Jyeshta
amavasya) came on Poorva Ashada Day. This was the first
Amavasya of the month of Margasira [at the beginning of
Sarad Ruthu, which began the year in Sri Krishna's time].
Hence Navarathri or Durga Pooja began the next day *[Just
2 years before on a similar holiday, Udhishtira performed
Durga Pooja, and on the Vijaya Dasami day, he performed
Ayudha Puja and then entered Virata Nagar]. On the 10th
day i.e Vijayadasami day, Ayudhapuja was performed
(U. Parva ch. 160 and 161).

*This Navarathri is termed *Sarada Navarathri* in the
Dharma Sastras. There is another called *Vasanta Navarathri*
celebrated at the begining of Vasanta Ruthu. Our present
Navarathri is celebrated at the beginning of Sarad Ruthu.

That evening Duryodana sent Uluka, son of Sakuni, to
the Pandavas His message and its delivery by Uluka are
very interesting reading. He told Sri Krishna and the
Pandavas that "Ayudha Puja is over today, Kurukshetra is
now dry and there is no reason for furthur delay in starting

the War". He demanded a straight reply from them. The Pandavas, on the advice of Sri Krishna, agreed to begin the war the next morning at sunrise. It was Sukla Ekadasi, Krittika Nakshatra of the month of Margasira, that the Bhagavad Gita was revealed by the Lord and Teacher of the three worlds, The War started at 6.30 A.M. (on Friday). Hence the 19th morning was Krishna Chathurdasi Thithi with Sravana Nakshatra.

(E) Bheeshma died at Midday on Magha Sukla Ashtami, Rohini Nakshatra. Reckoning from Jyeshta Amavasya, the number of days $= 29.53 \times 3 + 8 = 97$. The number of days from Jyeshta Amavasya to the beginning of the M.B. War $= 29.53 + 10 = 40$ days. Therefore the number of days from the beginning of M.B. War to Bheeshma's death both days inclusive $= 58$ days. This is referred to in the Santi Parva ch. 46 and the Anusasani Parva chap. 272.273 and 274, where in it is stated that "Bheeshma, who was in the bed of arrows, said, 'I have not slept for 58 days'." [as translated by Sriman Vidwan Melma Narasimha Thathacharya swamigal avl.] from the day he was made the General of the Kaurava Army.

(F) (i) *It is seen from the positions of the planets that the M.B. War was fought 38 years after the Astronomical Kali Era.*

(ii) The positions of the planets Sun, Moon and Rahu are now verified.

On the 10th Jan 3104 B.C. at about 5 P.M. the planets were as follows :—

Sun 312°37′ Moon 312°37′, Mercury 298°58′

Venus 298°16′, Mars 299°25′ Jupiter 299°10′

Saturn 299°5′ and Rahu 230°13′

(iii)

	Date B. C.	Julian Day	Week day	Sun	Rahu
New Moon	13-10-3105	587608	M¹ 1-87	225-27	235-25
Full Moon	28- 0-3105	587623	Tu 2-64	239-83	234-45
New Moon	12-11 3105	587638	W 3-40	254-39	233-64
~~Full~~ Moon	10- 1-3104	587697	S 6-46	312-61	230-22

13 Oct 3105 B.C. was Amavasya with Jyeshta Nakshatra, on Tuesday early morning. This is the then *Ritualistic Kali Yugadhi Day*, the beginning of the civil year of those times. The combination of (கேட்டை, முட்டை, செவ்வாய் கிழமை) Jyeshta, Amavasya on the early morning of Tuesday is considered very inauspicious, and it was with this that Kali Yuga began. On the next Full Moon day there was lunar eclipse visible in the early part of the night. [At 5 A.M. on 10.1.3104 B. C. the Astronomical Kali Yugadhi, the five planets were seen clustered together with the crescent Moon at Mid Shravishta]

(iv) 38 years after the beginning of the Astronomical Kali Era, i.e at the time of the Maha Bharata War, the positions of the planets were as follows :—

(a) Saturn :

168 cycles of saturn = $168 \times 10759.2198 = 1807642$ days.
4949 cyeles of sun = $4949 \times 365.25\ 689 = 1807656$ days.
∴ Saturn is behind sun by $0°.47$.

13th oct 3067 B. C. is 13023 Kaliday of L. N. Rao's Ephemeris (ie from 18-2-3102 B. C.)

∴ The corresponding Kaliday = $1807656 + 13023$ = 1820679 i.e Thurs 29 Nov 1883 A. D.

Hence Position of Saturn = 44.4+0.5 = 44.9 (Rohini) Since Saturn was in opposition, it was very bright.

(b) Sun and Moon :—

38 sidereal years = 38 × 365.25689 = 13879.7584 days

470 lunations = 470 × 29.5305 = 13879 3764 days

Difference = .382 day = 0°.377

∴ The position of Sun and Moon at New Moon was 225.27 − 0.377 = 224°.89

Note : The difference between the Zodiac of the Vedanga Jyotisha and that of the present Indian Government = 1°46' = 1°.77. Therefore the correct position of the Amavasya was 226.66 i.e. the beginning point of Jyeshta Nakshatra and also of the *Yoga Tara, Antares of Scorpio.*

The corresponding week day was 1.87 plus 5.38 = 0.26 − Sunday.

The newmoon thithi extended from the midday of Saturday to the midday of Sunday. Confusion was caused as to which day is Amavasya. This is revealed in the traditional story, that Sri Krishna made Saturday, the Amavasya day, while Duryodana thought Sunday, as Amavasya day. Many interesting religio—social and astronomical features are revealed by this story.

(c) Rahu :

Motion of Rahu in 38 years = 38 × 19.35548 = 15°.509

Therefore position of Rahu = 235°.25 − 15°.51 = 219°.74

On the day when Sri Krishna conversed with Karna, the Sun was at 218°, Rahu at 220°, (approaching the sun) and the Moon was coming from behind to overtake the Sun. Veda Vyasa's words are wonderfully true. It is also seen to be a solar eclipse day on Jyeshta Day.

Again tradition is that this Amavasya was a long thithi and so the next Poornima was a short thithi. On that day full moon ended at 0.25 plus 14.74=0.99 i.e. there were three thithis that Sunday. The day began with a Chaturdasi and ended with Krishna Prathama. This is the full moon before the Maha Bharata war, referred to by Sri Krishna in the Mousala Parva.

(d) On the Jyeshta day mentioned by Sri Krishna, in his conversation with Karna, the sun and the moon were at 225°. So on the Uthara Phalguni Day, the day of the conversation, the sun was at 218°and Rahu at 220°was approaching the sun, and the moon was approaching the sun from behind.

(e) Again during this time Mars was in Anuradha and Jyeshta. Thus the cruel planets Saturn, Mars, and Rahu were aspecting the sun and the moon, indicating a great war —Bheeshuna Parva.

(f) Jupiter was at Rohini with Saturn—Bheeshma Parva

(g) Solar eclipse is indicated on both the occasions just before the Maha Bharata War and before the Yadava civil war, 35 years after the M.B. war. It is stated that both amavasyas came on the 13th day. Again three thithis in a day is indicated by the words " Chathurdasi was made Poornima." These conditions are satisfied on the dates shown below This proves the correctness of the statements of Sri Veda Vyasa and the correct date of the M.B. War.

	Date B. C.	Julian Day	Week Day	Sun	Rahu	
New Moon	13–10–3067	601488	Sun 0–25	224–89	219–74	
Full Moon	27–10 3067	601502	Sun 0–99	239–46	218–93	
New Moon	11–11–3057	601517	Mon 1–78	254–02	218–13	
New Moon	11–12–3067	601547	Wed 3–31	283-15	216-52	

Special Note : The day following the Amavasya of 11 Nov. 3067 B.C. is the first Sukla ‚Prathama of the year, at the beginning of Margasira month and Sarad Ruthu [in Sri Krishna's time Margasira was the first month of the year]. Therefore Durga Pooja or Navarathri started on Tuesday 12th Nov. 3067 B.C. The tenth day was Vijaya Dasami Day i.e Ayudha Puja day. This is the day on which Duryodana sent Uluka to the Pandavas, asking them to start the war the next day. On the advice of Sri Krishna, the Pandavas agreed to it. Hence *the Maha Bharata War was started on Friday, Margasira month, Sukla Ekadasi Thithi, Krittika Nakshatra, 22 Nov. 3067 B. C.—601528 Julian Day,* Ekadasi ending at Fri. 5.60 and the Moon at 37.74 or Krittika on Friday morning. This is in complete accord with tradition.

CHAPTER V
The Date of the Rajasuya
and
The Beginning of the Yudhishtira Era

1. The Maha Bharata states that the Raja Suya was completed on the New Moon day with Jyeshta and Moola Nakshatras—Fifteen years before the M.B. War.

2. The Kala Bali or Field Sacrificial offering on the battle field of Kurukshetra was performed fifteen years after the Raja Suya.

3. The Field Sacrifice of the M. B. war was fixed on 13 Oct. 3067 B.C. Julian day 601488. Sunday. 25 New Moon Day with the sun at 224.89, But Sri Krishna had it done the previous midday.

4. 15 sidereal years = 5478.8520 days.
   185 lunations   = 5463.1610 days.
   Difference   = 15.69 days = $15°.47$

Therefore the position of Sun and Moon on the Raja Suya Day was $240°.36$.

The corresponding weekday $= 7.25 - 3.16 = 4.09$.
   i.e. Thursday, early morning.

The Julian Day $= 6014.88 - 5463.16 = 596024.84$
   $= 596025 -$ Thursday.

This day is Margasira Sukla Prathama, Moola Nakshatra, when the Yudhishtire Era was begun. i.e. 26 Oct. 3082 B.C.

5. Rajasuya coronation was the day before i.e. on Amavasya Day, with Jyeshta and Moola Nakshatras. Wednesday, Julian Day 596024, 25 Oct. 3082 B.C.

6. The Yudhishtira Era began on 26th Oct. 3082 B.C.

Date of exile and return of Pandavas

From a combined study of Sabha Parva and Virata Parva, it is easy to determine the dates of exile and return of the Pandavas-

(i) From the Sabha Parva, we learn that the game of dice was played about one year after the Rajasuya. The Pandavas were defeated, and sent out on condition that they should live in the forest for 12 years, and then in hiding for one more year. They accordingly left the place.

From the Virata, Parva chap 32, we learn that at the end of 13 years, in the month of Margasira (a) the Trigartas attacked the city of Virata, from the north, on Krishna Ashtami day, and (b) the Kaurava army attacked the city from the south on Krishna Navami day.

It was on this day that Arjuna revealed himself to the Kauravas. Immediately Duryodana, asked Bheeshma, if he had not come out earlier than the stipulated time, to which he replied that the Pandavas were in exile for 13 lunar years, five lunar months and 12 days ($=4766.42$ days) [13 sidereal years $=4748.34$ days, and so the Pandavas were in exile for 18 days more than the stipulated period].

Now the Pandavas were in exile for 13 lunar years, five lunar months and 12 days. Arjuna revealed himself on Krishna Navami. Therefore the exile began on Sukla Trayodasi day.

Let us now verify Veda Vyasa's reckoning of time.

(i) Rajasuya—Margasira Amavasya day with the sun at 241°Julian day <u>596024</u>

(ii) Next year—date of exile—Sukla Triyodasi day with the sun at $230+12=242°$, and Julian day $596024+29.53 \times 12+12\ 596 = 390.36 = \underline{596391}$

· (iii) 13 years later—Margasira Krishna Navami i.e. 4766.42 days later, with the sun at $260°$, Julian Day $= 596390.42+ 4766.42 = 601156.78 = \underline{601157}$

The exile began with the sun at $242°$. Therefore the Pandavas were in exile for 13 sidereal years $+18$ days.

(iv) One year later, at the beginning of the Maha Bharata war, on Margasira Sukla Ekadasi day i.e. $29.53 \times 12+17$ days later $= 371.36$ days later, the sun was at $265°$, and Julian day $601156.78+371.36 = 601528.14 = \underline{601528}$ th day

This is the day already determined from other independent data. Thus is revealed the truth of Veda Vyasa's astronomical data. Hence the date of exile was Julian day 596391 and the date of return $= 601157$ and the total period of exile $= 4766$ days $= 13$ sidereal years $+18$ days

CHAPTER VII

A few important events given in the Maha Bharata

See A.

1. Pandu died on the 14th birth day of Arjuna, at the beginning of the month of Madhava.

2. Just after Drona's war with Drupada, Yudhishtira was crowned Yuva Raja.

3. One year after Drona's war, Drowpathy was born.

4. The Pandavas went to Varanavatha in the month of Phalguna, Sukla Ashtami, Rohini Nakshatra. They entered the waxen palace 10 days later. Exactly one year later, the palace was set fire to on Krishna Chathurdasi night. After the fire incident, the Pandavas lived in hiding for 6 months in the Ashrama of Rishi Sali Hotra. Then they lived in Ekachakrapura for 7 months. Drowpathy's marriage follows.

5. A few months after the marriage, Yudhishtira was crowned king at Hastinapura. He rebuilt the city of Indraprastha and made it his Capital.

6. Nine years later, Rajasuya was celebrated on the New Moon day with Jyeshta and Moola Nakshatras.

7. Fifteen years later, the Field Sacrifice of the Maha Bharata war was performed on the New Moon Day with Jyeshta Nakshatra.

8. During the first day's battle of the M. B. War it is stated that the oldest warrior Bheeshma met the youngest warrior Abimanyu, who showed himself equal to the greatest warriors.

(ii) *5 months after the New Moon at 227.61 of this year.*

	Date B. C.	Julian Day	Week day	Sun
New Moon	15–10–3032	614274	Th 4–695	227–61
New Moon	12– 2–3031	614393	Th 4–215	344–13
New Moon	12– 3–3031	614422	F 5–345	13–26
Full Moon	27– 3–3031	614437	Sa 6–115	27–83

(a) In the afternoon of 13 Feb 3031 B.C. Julian Day 614394, Friday, Chaitra Sukla Prathama, Uthara Proshtapada Nakshatra Sri Krishna ascended to Heaven. The Yadava destruction was on the previous day, Amavasya day.

(b) The morning of 614436 Julian Day was Friday, 26 March 3031 B.C., Sukla Chathurdasi upto about 9 AM., and Poornima later. The moon was at Visakha (200° to 213⅓). Hence it was on this day that Sri Satagopa (Nammalwar) was born exactly the 43rd day after Sri Krishna's departure.

(c) The month of Vaisakh began on Saturday, 13 March 3031 B.C. i.e. 614423 Julian Day. The month of Chaitra began on Friday 12 Feb 3031 B.C. i.e. 614394 Julian Day. Sri Satagopa was born on Friday, 26 March 3031 B.C. i.e. 614436 Julian Day. i.e. he was born on the 43rd day of the year, from Chaitra Sukla Prathama. Thus it is true to the statement of "Edu", the famous commentary of the 1000 verses of Sri Satagopa.

Thus it is seen that these events agree entirely with traditional statements.

CHAPTER VI

Determination of the date of the Yadava Civil War, and the date of birth of Sri Satagopa :

(i) *35 years after the MahaBharata War i.e. at the time of the Yadava Civil War* :—

35 sidereal years = 12783.988 days
433 lunations = 12786.645 days
Difference = 2.757 days = $2^\circ.719$
Motion of Rahu = $35 \times 19.35548 = 317.44$
∴ Position of Rahu = $219.74 - 317.44 + 360 = 262^\circ.30$

	Date B.C.	Julian Day	Week day	Sun	Rahu
New Moon	15-10-3032	614274	Th 4-695	227-61	262-30
New Moon	14-11-3032	614304	Sa 6-225	256-74	260-69
Full Moon	29-11-3032	614319	Sa 6-995	271-31	259-89
New Moon	13-12-3032	614333	Sun 0-765	285-87	259-08

(a) Solar eclipse on 14 Nov 3032 B.C.

(b) Lunar eclipse on 29 Nov 3032 B.C., a day of three thithis, mentioned by Sri Krishna.

(c) N:te the similarity in the two cases mentioned by Sri Krishna. Rahu makes a solar eclipse and long thithis at the New Moon. The following full moon is a short thithi merged in between Sukla Chathurdasi and Krishna Prathama, on which day there are three thithis. The two phenomenon occurring together is a rare feature, and its repetition in in 35 years is again very rare.

9. Abimanya died just after completing his 16th year. His divine father Chandra, sent his son Varchas to be born as Abimanyu, with the express understanding that he should return on completing his 16th year.

10. Note on Subhadra's marriage and the birth of Abimanyu :—

In 3085 B.C. Arjuna had to go out on pilgrimage for 12 months. At the end of the period, when a few days were still left, he went to Dwaraka in the garb of a sanyasi and married Subhadra secretly with the help of Sri Krishna. The Yadava chiefs were asked by Sri Krishna to go to the Island and perform pujas to propitiate the Nava Grahas. 3084 B.C. is one of those very very rare years, when the three planets Saturn, Jupiter and Mars are together and retrograde [203, 200 and 179° resptly with the sun at 41°]—Refer Swami Kannu Pillai—Indian Ephemeris for this particular combination of planets in the year 3084 B.C.

Again the Gandharva Vivaha of Subhadra—Arjuna took place in the month of Vaisakha, Utharayana, Sukla Paksha *Thritheeya* (+10) Hasta Nakshatra, Bava Karana, Makara Lugna. This clearly shows that Arjuna married Subhadra in the month of Vaisakha of 3084 B.C. and Abimanyu was born in the month of *Magha* of 3083 B.C. On completing 16 years he died in the month of *Powshya* (or Makara) in the year 3067 B.C. during the M.B. War.

Section B.
Dates of a few important Events of the Maha Bharata—

Event	Sri Krishna's Age	Date B.C.
	Yrs—mth.	
1. Birthday of Sri Krishna	0–0	27 July 3112
2. Saptha Rishi Era—Beginning of 76th year of Magha Nakshatra— and beginning of Kali Era		23 Dec. 3106
3. Ritualistic and Civil Kali Era	7–168	11 Jan. 3104
4. Astronomical Kali Era		14 Oct. 3105
5. Pandavas entered Hastinapura	12–10½	July 3099
6. Drona's War with Drupatha— Yudhishtira's Yuva Rajyabishekam	18–3	Nov. 3094
7. Drowpathy's marriage	20–8	Ap. 3091
8. Yudhishtira's Rajyabishekam Re-building Indraprastha	21–3	Nov. 3091
9. Arjuna's Theertha Yatra begins	26–9	May 3085
10. Note: For 5½ yeas from Nov. 3085 B.C., Arjuna conquered and annexed all the adjacent Kingdoms and expanded the Kingdom of Yudhishtira. He earned the name of the greatest warrior of his times next to Sri Krishna.		
11. Subhadra's marriage	27–8	Ap. 3084
12. Burning of Gandava forest	27–11	July 3084
13. Birth of Abimanyu	28–6	Feb. 3083
14. Beginning of Rajasuya	29–3	Nov. 3083
15. End of Rajasuya and the crowning of Yudhishtira as Samrat	30–3	Wed. 25 Oct. 3082
16. Yudhishtira Era began	30–3	Thursday 26 Oct. 3082
17. Beginning of Vana Vasa	31–3	Nov. 3081
18. Maha Bharata War.	45–4	Friday 22 Nov. 3067
19. Yadava Civil War ends on New Moon day, Sri Krishna went to Heaven on Chaitra Sukla Prathama	80–9	Friday 13 Ap. 3031
20. Maha Prasthana of Pandavas.		Nov. 3031

APPENDIX

DEWAN BAHADUR SWAMIKANNU PILLAI, M.A.,B.L. AND THE MAHABHARATA

Mr. Pillai has made a number of unwarranted remarks about the Maha Bharata and Sri Veda Vyasa, with regard to the many astronomical references found in the MahaBharata. Herein I quote a few of them, and then show that Sri Veda Vyasa was perfectly correct in all his observations.

(1) **Indian Ephemeris Vol. 1 Part 1. by D. B. S. K. Pillai Page 8 :** "In this connection reference may be made to the hallucination that a lunar fortnight with only 13 days does not occur except once in 1000 years. In the Maha Bharata, Bheeshma Parva (3—32), it is recounted by Vyasa in the course of his convesation with Dhritarashtra, that he has known of lunar fortnights consisting of 14, 15 or 16 days, but never of one consisting of 13 days, but since such a one is in prospect or has occurred, there will be a great slaughter of human beings. Other sastras quoted by Dr. Fleet in Indian Antiquary Vol XIV for March 1887, reiterate this omen, and it is stated in one of the quotations (commentary of Muhurta Ganapathi) that the phenomenon occurs only once in 1000 years. But it is not true that the phenomenon takes place only once in a 1000 years...comment is needless".

Again referring to the same sloka, he makes the following remarks in page 483—" 2 eclipses one solar and the next lunar succeeding each other within a fortnight is quite an ordinary phenomenon"

The concerned verse is—

"Chaturdas'im, panchadas'im, bhūta pūrvām cha shodas'im/Imāmtu nā bi janami amavasyam trayodasim".

Bheeshma Parva—3— 32

"Chandra surya vubhau grasta vekahne hi trayodas'im‖
aparvani grahâ vetau prajâ samshaya yishyatah"

Bheeshma Parva—3—32

Meaning :

"A lunar fortnight has hitherto consisted of 14 days or
15 days or 16 days. Up to now I have not known of amavasya
coming on the 13 th day"—

"But on the 13th day and in the course of the same
month two eclipses have taken place, So there will be a
great slaughter of human beings."

Now we easily understand what Sri Veda Vyasa said to
Dritarashtra and we can see how Mr. Pillai has cut the
slokas. It is true that 13 days fortnights are not rare, and
and 2 eclipses in a fortnight are also not rare. But can any
one point out *a 13 day fortnight with 2 eclipses in a month.*

Moreover a month means a lunar month, and amavasya
is the last day of the month. Hence the eclipses must be
lunar followed by solar, and not the other way as Mr. Pillai
understands.

This one is therefore an extra—ordinarily rare
phenomenon. Such a one occurred in the month of Krittika,
just before the Maha Bharata war with a lunar eclipse followed
by a solar eclipse.

The language and tone of Mr. Pillai's expression show
his arrogance and reveal a sense of scoffing at Veda Vyasa

(2) **Indian Ephemeris Vol I Part I by Sri S. K. Pillai
Page 99 :** "When exactly the people of this country became
acquainted with the names of the other planets (for the sun
and the moon are also planets in the Indian system) or began
to observe their motions is a moot point. On the one hand

5

it seems apriori probable, from the intercourse of this country with the western nations from very ancient times, that Greek if not Phoenician, Chaldean, and Egyptian astronomy and astrology must have found their way into this country at a very early time. It seems difficult to suppose that Chaldean astrology in particular, which was practised in the Grecian and Roman states for some centuries before A. D. 1., did not find its way into India in the wake of Alexander's conquest or of the Graeco-Bactrian civilisation. Indeed in an account of the life of Apollonius of Tyana, who lived in the first century A. D. it is stated that he became acquainted with the names of the planets and of the week-days from an Indian Prince whom he visited, but there is reason to believe that the extant semi-mythic accounts of the life of Apollonius of Tyana were composed considerably later than the first century A. D.

All the historical, as distingiushed from the presumptive evidence that has come down to us points to the probability of western influence on Indian planetary astronomy not having been anterior to the fourth or fifth century A.D. when the great Greek astronomer and astrologer Klaudios Ptolemy and his successors Paulus Alexandrinus and Firmicus Maternus were first introduced into this country during the Gupta Period. Some mention is made of planet names in the Puranas, but the date of composition of the Puranas is itself a matter of critical speculation. On the whole it may be safe to presume that the Hindus in some way became acquainted with the names of the planets, and possibly of the planetary week days, a century or two before the christian era, but that they did not make any practical use of this knowledge until they were brought face to face with its results in Ptolemy's works in the fourth or fifth century A.D. It seems also exceedingly probable that the practice of calculating horoscopes or the positions of the planets at given moments. came into vogue in India, a century or two after the fifth A.D,..."

At the time of the Maha Bharata war, [whatever date the western scholars may fix for it] the Greeks were a wild nude tribe roaming the forests of Eastern Europe. The many aceurate astronomical referenecs to planets in the Maha Bharata show the difference in stature between these wild tribes and the highly cultured Aryas of Bharat Varsha-

Mr. Pillai thinks that Hindus classified the Sun and Moon as planets—what ignorance! Valmiki Sundarakanda—"Graha, Nakshatra, Chandra, Arka, Tara gana" meaning "planets, lunar mansions, moon, sun, and constellations." There are many references in the Rig Veda to this effect.

Again Mr. Pillai assumes the names of the planets came to India in early A. D. years What about the innumerable references to planets in the M. B. Mr. Pillai seems to outwit even Max Muller

(3) Indian Ephemeris Vol I Part 1. by Mr Pillai

(i) **Page 100, para 246 :** "The obvious inaccuracies in the M. B. references to planets will be commented on in an Appendix (Paper No. 5)"

(ii) **Pages 479 and 480:**—" The popular impression concerning these references is that the observations in question were made at the time of occurrence of the events described in the M. B., while the pious hope of even the well informed portion of readers and hearers of the M. B. is that it may be possible by means of these references, to determine the date of those events or atleast of the composition of the poem...... There is absolutely no scientific or historic warrant for either the popular impression or the pious hope. The astronomical details given in the Maha Bharata differ in one respect from those in the Ramayana...; where as the Maha Bharata cannot possibly yield a date because (i) they are mutually repugnant as has been stated already at page 100 of the text, (ii) they are the evident result of interpolation by subsequent writers and (iii) they seem to have been interpolated at different times and in different centuries A. D.

(iii) Page 481 :—" Some of the Maha Bharata references to astronomy afford an even better illustration of *reckless astrological statements made without due regard to astronomicalt possibilities* "

The author then continues to discuss the retrograde motion of Mars, Saturn and Jupiter. He suggests that Mars Jup. and Saturn were retrograde near Visakha. He then proceeds to give possible dates for this. How is this possible in Margasira month, well known as the month of the Mahabharata War ?

The above are the remarks of the anglicised outlook of an Indian Christian. It would have been better if he had confined himself to chronology, and not meddled with the sacred literature of the Hindus ego the Ramaya na, the Mahabharata, the Guruparampara of the Alwars, ete.

The purpose of this paper is to show that Sri. Veda Vyasa wrote down what he saw, and that all the astronomical references in the Maha Bharata are consistent and true, and the remarks of Sri. S. K. Pillai are unwarranted.

Before reviewing Mr. Pillai's remarks on the Maha Bharata Verses, a few important points regarding Indian Jyotisha must be clearly understood.

(i) There are 3 sections in Jyotisha Sastra

(a) Samhita   (b) Hora   (c) Ganita.

(a) In the Samhita, the effects of planets and other celestial phenomena on countries and peoples are given in detail.

(b) In the Hora, the effects on individuals is discussed, based on their time of birth.

(c) In the Ganita is given the methods of calculation to fix the position of the planets etc.

Veda Vyasa and his father Maha Rishi Parasara are considered very great scholars in Jyotisha, and so these three aspects are indicated here, and Veda Vyasa gives his reading of the planets, comets, etc.

(ii) Again according to Indian Jyotisha, there are many Ketus. A reference to Brihat Samhita by Varaha Mihira will clarify this point. Therefore when Veda Vyasa mentions a Ketu, we should know what he refers to. It should not be assumed that Ketu is the 180th degree position of Rahu. This kind of ketu is not at all mentioned by Veda Vyasa any where in the Maha Bharata.

(iii) Mr. Pillai does not seem to understand the meaning of the words "Peedyathe" and "Vakra". Though an Indian, he does not seem to understand what every Hindu knows.

When an eclipse occurs in the Rohini Nakshatra, the Panchang clearly states that Peeda Parihara (ceremonies to avert peeda) must be performed by those whose Nakshatras are Rohini, Hasta and Sravana, and the Nakshatras adjacent to these 3 Nakshatras. In the days of Maha Bharata the 12 Rasis were unknown. The 27 Nakshatras alone were in vogue. The Nakshatras were grouped in threes eg Aswin, Magha, Moola ; Barani, Poorva Phalguni, Poorva Ashada; .. A malefic planet or comet in any one of the Nakshatras is said to have malefic aspect on the other two of the triad, directly on one and retrogradely on the other. This retrograde malefic aspect is named "Vakra Peedyathe"

(iv) On the Kala Bali (Field sacrifice) day i.e 13 Oct 3067 B.C. The planets were in the following positions :—

Sun, Moon, Mars, Venus, Rahu and⌒ in *Jyeshta*, Jupiter, Saturn and r in *Rohini*.

Doomadhi Paneha Grahas—Dooman 358°20', Vyatheepathan—Vakra 1°40'

Pari Vesham 181°40' (Vakra) ⎫
Indra Dhanus 178°20' ⎬ Chitra and Swathi
Dooma Ketu 195° ⎭

(v) At the beginning of the Maha Bharata War i.e on 22 Nov 3067 B.C., the planets were in the following positions:

Sun : Poorva Ashada.

Moon : Krittika.

Mer : Jyeshta.

Venus : End of Anuradha

Mars : Moola.

Jupiter : Rohini.

Saturn : Rohini.

Rahu : Jyeshta.

Υ = Vernal Equinox : Rohini

⌒ = Autumual Equinox : Jyeshta

(vi) Mr. Pillai is assertive when he says that many interpolations have been made at different times. But so far as the astronomical details are concerned. they are consistent and no one seems to have meddled with Veda Vyasa's verses. It is his unwillingness to understand them properly that is the cause of his statement.

(vii) In the light of the above basic ideas, let us now study Mr. Pillai's translations and remarks on the Maha Bharata verses :—

(4) Indian Ephemeris Vol I part I Appendix V page 479 Astronomical references in the M.B.

(1) Bheeshma Parva—ch.2 Verse 23

Alakshe prabaya hinam paurnamasimcha Kartikim
Chandro bhudogni varnascha padme varnenabhastale ||

Even in the night of the Kartika full moon, the moon having lost all its splendour became invisible (or looked like fire), the sky looking like lotus.

(2) Bheeshma Parva ch.2. Verse 32

Rohanim pidayan-mesha sthito rajan Sanais'charah|
Vyavrittam lakshma somasya bhavishyati mahabhayam ||

O ! King, the planet Sani oppresses Rohini. *The sign of the deer in the moon* has shifted from its position. A great evil is foreboded by all this.

(3) Bheeshma Parva chap 3, verse 12

Sveto grahastatha *chitram* samatikramya tishthati |
abhavam hi viseshena Kurunam tatra pasyati ||

Ketu, the white planet stops on passing beyond the constellation chitra. All this forebodes total destruction of the Kurus.

(4) Bheeshma Parva chap. 3 Verse 13

Dhumaketuh maha ghorah pushyam chakramya tishthathi ! senayorasivam ghoram karishyati maha ghorahah||

A fearful comet is rising and is distressing Pushya ; this great planet will cause great havoc to both armies.

(5) Bheeshma parva—chap 3 verses 14 to 16.

Maghasvangarako vakkrah sravanecha brihaspatih |
Bhagam nakshatra makramya suryaputrena pidyate ||

Sukra proshta pada purve samaruhya virochate |
uttaretu parikramya sahitah samudikshyate ||

Sveto grahah prajvalitah saduma iva pavakah |
endram tejasvi nakshatram jyeshtam akramya tishtathi |

Mars is retrograde in Magha, and Brihaspathy in Sravana. The sun's off spring Sani advances towards Bhaga and afflicts l The planet sukra rises towards Purva Bhadra (Dutt's translation) l *Keta* blazing like smoky fire, stops and afflicts the effulgent constellation of Indra l

(6) Bheeshme parva-ch 3 verse 17
Dhruvah prajvalitho ghoramapasaviyam pravartate l
Rohinim pidayantau tauabhau cha Sasi bhaskrau ll
chitra svatyantare chaiva dhishthatah parusha grahah l

The consiellation Dhruva, fearfully blazing advances towards the right. Both the sun and the moon distress Rohini. A terrible planet (Rahu) has taken up its position between Chitra and Swathi.

(7) Bheeshma Parva—ch 3-verse 18.
Vakranuwakram Kritvacha Sravanam Pavaka prabhah ll
brahma rasim samavritya lohitango vyavasthitah ll

The red bodied planet, effulgent like fire passing in a round and round way stops encircling Sravana over ridden by Brihaspathy ll

(8) Bheeshma Parva—ch 3-verse 27.

Samvatsara sthayrnau cha grahau prajvalita vubhau l
[vis'akhayah sami pasthau] brihaspati s'anais-charau ll

The two burning planets Brihaspati and S'ani have become fixed for a year.

(9) Bheeshma Parva—ch 3-verse 29.

Krittikam pidayanstikshnaih nakshatram prithvipate l
abhikshnavata vayante dhumaketu mavasthitah ll

O king ! Rahu of terrible deeds afflicts krittika. Rough winds, foreboding terrible danger, are continually blowing.

(10) Bheeshna Parva—ch 3–verse 32.

Chathurdasim panchadasim bhutapurvam cha shodasiml imamtu nabhi janami amavasyam trayodasim ||

(11) Bheeshma Parva—ch 3–verse 33.

Chandras surya vubhau grastavekahne hi trayodasim | aparvani graha vetau praja samkshaya yishyatah ||

A lunar fortnight has hitherto consisted of 14 days or 15 days or 16 days. But on the 13th day and in the course of the same month two eclipses have taken place,

(12) Udyoga Parva—chap 142–verse 18.

Saptamaccapi divasat amavasya bhavishy ati | sangramo yujyatham tasyam tamahuh sakra devatam ||

In seven days there will be *full moon*, and on that day let us engage in fight, for that is the day favourite to Sakra.

(13) Udyoga Parva—ch 143–verse 8.

Prajapatyam hi nakshatram grahastikshmo maha dyratih | Sanaischarah pidayati pidayan pranino adhika ||

That active planet of great effulgence, Sani, troubles the star Prajapatya, indicating greater trouble to living creatures.

(14) Udyoga Parva—ch. 143–

Krikva changarako vakram Jyeshthayam madusudana || anuradham prarthayate maitram sangamayanniva ||

The planet Angaraka travels retrograde to the constellation Jyeshta, 0! slayer of Madhu, and goes towards Anuradha as if seeking its friendship.

(15) Nunam mahad bhayam krishna Kurunam, samupasthi tham | Viseshena hi Varshneya chitram pidayate grahah ||

Surely O ! Krishna, a great calamity for the Kurus is at hand, especially as the planets go against Chitra.

6

16. Somasya lakshma vya vrittam Rahurarka mupaitichaṭ divas' cholkah patantyetah sanirghata sakampanah ‖

Rahu comes to the sun which has covered the path of the moon, and from the heavens fall down meteors with loud noise and making the earth shake.

[first line is not translated]

1. **Correct interpretation of the above verses :**

This is a beautiful description of the lunar eclipse in the month of Krittika. Immediately after the rains, the sky is clear and usually the full moon is beautiful. In the words of Kalidasa—" Mahi shacha sarach chandra chandrika davalam dadhi"—the moonlight is white and dense like buffalo curd.

Mr. Pillai assumes that the lunar eclipse followed the solar eclipse in the month of Margasira. It is not so.

The field sacrifice at Kurukshetra was on 13 Oct 3067 B.C. New Moon—601488 Julian day—Sunday 0.25, with the sun and moon at 224.89 and Rahu at 219.74. It was a solar eclipse day with the eclipse at Midday.

The previous full moon was on 28 Sep 3067 B.C. 601473 Julian day—Saturday 6.51 with the sun at 210°.32 and Moon at 30°.32 and Rahu at 220°.55. It was a lunar eclipse day, with the eclipse immediately after sun set (moonrise).

Hence the description is that the moon lost its *usual brilliance of a Krittika full moon* and became invisible and the evening sky looked like red lotus. Maha Rishi Veda Vyasa's words are not mere poetic fancy, but a fact of observation.

In the Udyoga Parva it is said that Sri Krishna left for Hastinapura on his peace mission on the Revati day

Kartika month. He was therefore in Hastinapura on the full moon Krittika day, and returned to the Pandavas on Chitra Day.

(2) Saturn in Rohini :

(i) It is already shown that Saturn was in Rohini at the time of the M.B. War. Saturn in Rohini is considered very inauspicious for the whole country. This is seen in the Saneeswara sthothra of Emperor Dasaratha. It is no wonder that Veda Vyasa recalls this ancient tradition here.

(ii) The translation here is not correct. Even a layman knows that the sign of the Deer in the Moon is fixed. To assume that Veda Vyasa did not know this is nothing short of nonsense.

"Lakshma" means "the special and characteristic beauty of the Moon's lustre" Vyavrittam" means "is not as it should be".

In this sloka Veda Vyasa does not give the reason for this change. But in the 16th verse quoted by Mr. Pillai, the same line occurs again—"Somasya lakshma vyavrittam". Here in Vyasa gives the reasons—"The Sun and Rahu approach the Moon and there is a good meteoric shower" Is this not enough to prove the translation is incorrect ? The astrological reading is "bhavishyati Maha bhayam".

(3) Here again the translation is wrong- "Sveto graha" can never mean "Ketu". In books of Astrology "Ketu" is described as "dhumravarne" i.e smoky in colour. Again at the time of Veda Vyasa there was no planet "Ketu" as we mean today.

The South Indian reading is "Budho graha". This reading is correct. A referenee to "Budha", the first parent of the Lunar Race, changing his direct motion to retrograde and back again to direct motion while passing Chitra

Nakshatra is very interesting. Chitra Nakshatra is associated with the Lunar Race in a number of places in the Maha Bharata. This motion of Budha in Chitra foreboded the total destruction of the Kurus.

(4) "Dhuma Ketu maha gorah"—Any one who saw the Halley's comet in 1910, can easily recognise this "maha gorah" can mean only the great Dhuma Ketu, Halley's Comet.

It appeared in the following years (according to text books of astronomy) 1066, 1145, 1301, 1456, 1531, 1607, 1682, 1759, 1835 and 1910 A.D. Its period is 75 years 5 months. 66 revolutions before 1910 A.D. it was 3067 B. C. Hence at the time of the Maha Bharata war Halley's comet was in the sky. The appearance of this comet usually forebodes the death of a great king and a great war.

The Comet being close to the Sun (and slightly ahead of it) was in opposition to Pushya. [Sun at 267 and Comet at 275 to 285 was in opposition to Pushya $93°\frac{1}{3}$ to $106°\frac{2}{3}$]. Veda Vyasa's observation was correct. The Comet was shining fiercely in the evening sky.

(5) Not understanding the correct meaning of the words "Vakra" and "Peedyathe", the entire verse was wrongly translated and has caused confusion in the mind of Mr. Pillai. The verse is about the aspect called Vedhai [வேதை].

The correct meaning is as follows :—

(i) Maghasvangarako Vakrah peedyathe—Angaraka (from Moola) malefically aspects Magha in the retrograde aspect.

(ii) Sravanecha Brihaspathi, *vakra peedyathe*—Jupiter (from Rohini) malefically aspects Sravana in the retrograde aspect.

(iii) Bagham nakshatra makramya Surya putrena peedyathe—Saturn (from Rohini) directly aspects Uthara Phalguni.

(iv) Sukra—Venus—was at the end of Anuradha. Hence it was at its greatest elongation, and so shining brilliantly in the eastern sky before sunrise. From Anuradha it was afflicting Poova Proshtapada and moving to Jyeshta it was aspecting Uthara Proshtapada.

(v) Sveto graha—is Budha and not Ketu. It was in Jyeshta, Indra's Nakshatra, which was shining brilliantly.

(6) Both Venus and Mercury were shining brilliantly in the Eastern sky before sunrise and they were at Jyeshta with Rahu. The word "Dhruvah" meaning "stationary" refers to Mercury, the Sveto graha of the previous verse, which was moving in the retrograde direction (near the stationary position) and which was shining brilliantly because of its maximum elongation. The next line refers to Budha which was stationary between chitra and swathi (vide verse 3) a few months before.

(7) The Red bodied planet—Saturn—was aspecting Sravana Nakshatra, retrograde aspect from Rohini. The same sravana was also aspected by Brihaspathy (Jupiter) from Rohini.

(8) It is correct to say the Jupiter and Saturn would stay together (at Rohini) for a year.

(9) Rahu at 218° directly aspects 218—180=30° i.e. Krittka. The effect of this is described as foreboding rough winds

(10) and (II) Mr. Pillai wastes his energy by pointing out a number of years when a fortnight was of 13 days. But that is not the point. He should not cut the sloka. Veda Vyasa states *that 2 eclipses have occurred at an interval of 13 days in the course of the same month.* This is a very rare

phenomenon. It may be difficult to find a parallel.—[Refer essay on M.B. war)

(12) Sri Krishna while leaving Hastinapura had a private conversation with Karna (on the Uthara phalguni day). Therein he states, "on the 7th day (Jyeshta) Amavasya is coming". This is discussed in detail in the main essay. The translation *full moon* is wrong.

(13) Saturn in Rohini—fully discussed earlier.

(14) Angaraka at Moola aspects Jyeshta (in retorgrade). This is the correct meaning. and has his malefic influence at Anuradha.

(15) When Karna made this statement, three of the five Doomadhi Pancha grahas were at Chitra as shown in 3) and Budha was stationary at chitra : Sun 225. Dooman 358°20 Vyatheepatham (Vakra) 1°40' Pari Vesha (Vakra) at 181°40', Indra Danus 178°20'. Dooma Ketu 195°. the three last ones at Chitra and Swathi.

(16) On the day mentioned by Sri Krishna, Rahu was moving towards the sun in front and the moon was moving towards the sun from behind. This is fully discussed in the main essay. (cf. sl. 2. discussed already).

As the earth was moving in the region of the meteoric Radiant, there was a heavy downpour of meteors. Possibly at that time, it was the densest part of the Meteoric showers.

———

Determination of the date of the Astronomical Kali Yuga Era

———

A. From 1690 A.D. Bailey Bentley. Burgess, Colebrooke, Cunningham. Davis, Delambre, Laplace, Playfair, Sewell, Thibaut, Wallis, Warren, Weber, Whyte and many western scholars took interest in the Indian system of Astronomy, and began to study them. Some of them ascribed great antiquity and originality to the Indian system, while others maintained it was all borrowed from the Greeks.

This stalemate went on till 1800 A. D., when Bentley worked out the initial date of ǀKali Yuga Era, the starting point of Indian chronology. He fixed the date of Kali Yugadhi at 18 Feb 3102 B.C. He then worked out the position of the planets on that day by modern astronomical methods. *According to Indian Tradition Astronomical Kali Yuga began with the 5 planets together, at the initial point of the Zodiac.* But Bentley showed that they were disposed as follows : Sun 351°, Moon 355, Mercury 318° Venus 24° Mars 340° Jupiter 8° and Saturn 332° [the Zero point of the Zodiac is at 180° from Spica, Chitra Nakshatra]. He also showed that the error decreased from 3102 BC to 500 A.D. and then increased. He therefore concluded that Kali Yugadhi was only a myth and an extra polated date by Indian astronomers of 500 A.D. Immediately all the western scholars joined to condemn Indian tradition and the Indians in a " vulgar and vituperative language ".

Thus on this slender evidence they concluded that Kali Yugadhi was a myth and Veda Vyasa, a mythical person, and that Indian astronomers borrowed everything from the Greeks after 300 B. C. Thereafter it was easy for them to write the history of India from their own distorted vision of Indian antiquity.

1. Now a reference to Indian Panchang (Almanac) shows Kali Yugadhi marked on Magha Sukla Prathama day (the first day of the bright half of the lunar month, Magha). This is corroborated by the Vedanga Jyotisha verses, that state that the Vedic Yuga of 5 years should always begin with the year Samvatsara on Magha Sukla Prathama (Vide B. G. Tilak and others). But western chronologists took Meshadi as the beginning of the then Indian sidereal year, and therefore of Kali Yugadhi, not knowing that this was fixed by the Siddhanta Astronomers of the early A. D. years.

This was the first error they committed.

2. Again, the first year of the present Kali series (beginning on 18.2. 3102 B. C.) is seen to be Anuvatsara, the 4th year of the 5 year Yuga of Vedanga Jyotisha. Therefore the Yuga began three years earlier with the Magha Sukla Prathama on Sunday 23 Dec. 3106 B. C.

This was the second error they committed.

3. Moreover, it was at the next Magha Sukla Prathama, the astronomical Kali Yuga began, on Sunday 11 Jan. 3104 B. C., (26 lunations before 18. 2. 3102 B. C.), because *at 5 P. M. on Saturday 10 Jan 3104 B.C., the five planets Mercury, Venus, Mars, Jupiter and Saturn were at 300° (Mid Shravishta—the initial point of the Zodiac of Vedanga Jyotisha), with the Sun and Moon at 314°.*

Mr. Bentley who laboriously worked out the positions of the planets from 18.2. 3102 B. C. to 1800 A. D. to prove that Indian Tradition was false, failed to go back by 26 lunations. Had he done so, he would have recognised the truth and correctness of the Traditional statement.

Thus the theory of modern chronologists that Kali Yugadhi is a myth and an extrapolated date is disproved, and the great antiquity of Hindu Astronomy is established.

I shall now enunciate a few convenient conventions before discussing the subject :—

(i) For fixing the position of celestial objects tropical longitudes and latitudes are usually employed. But this is very misleading for purpose of comparison. Hence I propose to adopt a fixed Zodice. The present Indian Government Calendar was fixed on 21st March 1956 A. D. and the corresponding saka year = 1878 (78+expired saka years=A. D. years). The beginning of the Indian year now follows the precessional motion of the Vernal Equinox. But the Zodiac is a fixed one, with Spica (chitra Nakshatra) at 180°. It is with reference to this zodiac, that I propose to give the position of the celestial objects. The Vedic Rishis adopted the same method and their fixed zodiac began with the midpoint of Shravishta. I have shown in another paper that the Govt. of India is in error by 1°46′ as compared to Vedic Zodiac.

(ii) Since the mean position of the planets is meaningless and misleading. I propose to give their actual apparent positions.

(iii) According to the Rishis, there are only five planets : Mercury, Venus, Mars, Jupiter and Saturn. The sun and the Moon are not classified with them as they have no retrograde and lateral motion. Ref. (a) Valmiki Ramayana— Sundara Kanda Chap. 1 Verse 191. " *Graha, Nakshatra, Chandra, Arka, Taragana* nishevite. (5 Planets, 27 Nakshatras, Moon Sun and the many constellations). (b) Rig Vedic Samhita X 55-4″ Indra, he filled the two worlds, and what is between in manifold ways. He looks at the 5 gods, with 34 fold lights of one colour but different laws", Vedic scholars Prof Hildebrandt, Prof Ludwig and others have interpreted it as the sun, the moon the 5 planets and the 27 Nakshatras (c) R. S I-105-10 (d) R. S. III 7-7, "Five Advaryus (planet) moving hither and thither in a Yagna"—(e) Taitriya Samhita-"Prajapthy giving 33 daughters in marriage to Soma"—Prof. Zimmerman interprets this as 5 planets, 27 Nakshatras and the divine being Surya.

(iv) The method used for calculating the positions of the planets is that of Sri L. Narayana Rao M.A. given in his book "Perpetual Ephemeris of the planetary cycles". I have slightly altered it and improved it. It is a better method than the one given by Dewan Bahadur Swami Kannu Pillai in his "Indian Ephemeris" I give this method because it is easy to understand. I have verified the results by the difficult dynamical formula and the diffenence is not greater than 15'. The correctness of the method is also verified by calculating the positions of the planets on 21 st March 499 AD, 1st January 1800 A.D., 1st Jan, 1900 A.D. and 1st Jan. 1968 A. D.

(v) Calculations are made for midday position ; but week days are reckoned from sunrise at Kurukshetra 30°N 77°E (i.e. 5 Hours 8' in advance of Greenwich). Ujjain (Avanti) is 23°N, 75¾°E (i.e. 5 Hours 3' in advance of Greenwich).

(i) From the Vedic age up to the A.D. years, time was reckoned in terms of the luni solar months, the luni solar years and the yuga of 5 years defined by the Vedanga Jyotisha. The 27 Nakshatras marked the divisions of the zodiac. It was only after the influence of the pure solar reckoning of chaldeans and other western Asian cultures, the 12 Houses or Rasis of the zodiac were introduced. The Indian Nakshatra zodiac was a *fixed one*, beginning with Mid-Sravishta, while the other had its initial point fixed by the vernal Equinox, and hence it was *not a fixed zodiac*. The Vedic Rishis had the 12 solar months differently named. Their civil year was based on the Ruthus or seasons, while their astronomical year was based on the fixed zodiac.

(ii) The astronomical Kali Yugadhi of Veda Vyasa was associated with the Sravishta Nakshatra, *Magha Sukla Prathama*. In fixing the date Varaha Mihira used the Aharghana of Indian Astronomers i.e. the number of days expired from the beginning of *Kali Yuga* to his date. But in so doing, the length of the year taken by him was slightly in error, and consequently. The position of the sun and the moon on that day was slightly wrong. Bentley taking the same Aharghana fixed Kali Yugadhi with modern astronomical constants on Friday the 18th Feb. 3102 B. C., Dewan Bahadur Swami Kannu Pillai, the Calender Reform Committe of the Government of India, and other scholars of Europe and India have adopted the same method. But they all disagree about the moment and position of *Mesha* Sukla Prathama on Friday 18th Feb. 3102 B. C. But they all agree about the *Chaitra Sukla Prathama* Thithi of Friday 18th Feb. 3102 B. C. The cause of the difference is due to the different values of the sidereal year taken by them.

Note :   Sravishta ranges from $293\frac{1}{3}°$ to $306\frac{2}{3}°$

Magha Sukla Prathama begins from the moment the sun and the moon have the same longitude in the range 285° to 315°. Mesha Sukla Prathama begins when the New Moon ends in the range— —15° to +15°.

Starting with the Vernal Equinox at 6 A. M. on 21st March 499 A.D. and the Aharghana of the day = 1314932, they used the following values for the length of the sidereal year—

1. Surya Siddhanta   —365 days 15g 26k
2. Vakya Siddhanta   —365 days 15g 31k 15¼ V. K.
3. Swami Kannu Pillai   —365.258756484 days
4. Lalande's Value used   —365 days 6 hours 12′ 9″
   by Bentley   —365 25636242 days
5. Nautical Almanac   —365.25636242 days
6. Newcomb   —365.2568984 days

Checking the error between Bentley and Varaha Mihira.

Difference in the length of the sidereal year = .0023182 days

Dif. in 3600 years = 8° 23'.   This is Bentley's figure on the Varaha Mihira's Zodiac of 499 A.D. This is—18° 21' on the Zodiac of 285 A.D. adopted by the Government of India.

This error accumulates negatively before 499 A.D. and positively after 499 A.D.   It is about this that Bentley made a big fuss, and claimed it as a positive proof of Varaha Mihira borrowing everything from the Greeks.   This error according to the Government of India is—9°40' on the Zodiac of 499 A. D. or—12° 38' on the zodiac of 285 A. D. This error according to S. K. Pillai is + 2° 10' on the Zodiac of 499 A. D. or—0° 48' on the zodiac of 285 A. D. One more point to be noted is that these astronomers have taken the mean position of the sun and the moon and not the actual apparent positions.

Working the same problem from the moment of New Moon nearest to (O Jan 1854 A.D. or O Jan. 1900 A.D. or) O Jan 1968 A.D. I have obtained the correet value as—10° 37' on the Zodiac of 285 A. D.

	Zodiac of 499 A. D.	Zodiac of 285 A. D,
Bentley	−8° 23'	−11° 21'
Lahiri	−9° 40'	−12° 38'
S. K. Pillai	+2° 10'	− 0° 48'
K. Sri	−7° 39'	−10° 37'

III The following astronomical data are necessary for the calculation and verification of the detailed work given later.

(A)

Christian Date	Julian Day	Kaliday from 18 2.3102 B. C.	Week Day	Ayanamsa
1 Jan. 1968 A.D.	2439857	1851392	Monday	23° 24' 29"
1 Jan. 1900 A.D.	2415021	1826556	Monday	22° 28'
21 Mar. 499 A.D.	1903397	1314932	Sunday	2° 58' 4"
22 Mar. 285 A.D.	1825235	1236770	Sunday	0° 0' 0"
18 Feb. 3102 B.C.	588466	1	Friday	−46° 34' 35"
11 Jan. 3104 B.C.	587698	−768	Sunday	−46° 36' 34"
13 Dec. 3105 B.C.	587669	−797	Saturday	
23 Dec. 3106 B.C.	587313	−1153	Sunday	−46° 38'
8581 B.C.			Sunday	−120³ 28'

(B) Sidereal year = 365. 2563624248 (N. A.) days,
        = 365. 2568984 (Newcomb) days.

Lunation or the synodic period of the moon
        = 29. 530587946 days.

Note : Newcomb's value of the sidereal year gives correct values for determining Magha Sukla Prathama, calculated for over 10000 years, as shown in the 2 worked examples of the book. It also agress very well with 5476th year of S. R Era

    Sidereal period of the Moon = 27. 3216615 days
        ,,   ,,   Mercury = 87.967608   ,,
        ,,   ,,   Venus   = 224.701786   ,,
        ,,   ,,   Mars   = 686'979645   ,,
        ,,   ,,   Jupiter = 4332'58482   ,,
        ,,   ,,   Saturn = 10759.219817   ,,

(c) Apparent position of the sun, moon, and planets at Greenwich on Monday O Jan. 1968 A. D. at midnight = 2439857 Julian day = 1851392 Kaliday, on the Indian Zodiac.

Sun	256° 12' 13"
Moon	267° 32' 18"
Mars	300° 01' 45"
Mercury	257° 59' 50"
Jupiter	132° 17' 00"
Venus	215° 27' 50"
Saturn	342° 41' 56"
Rahu	0° 35' 10"
Ayanamsa	23° 24' 29"

(D) Bentley and Lahiri have given the mean position, while the correct apparent positions at Kurukshetra are given here.

Position of the Sun and Moon at midnight on Thursday/ Friday 17/18 Feb. 3102 B.C., and the exact time of New Moon on Thursday 17 Feb. 3102 B.C. and the then position of the sun and moon are given below :—

	Midnight Th/Fri 17/18 Feb 3102 B.C.		Moment of New Moon on Th. 17 Feb. 3102 B.C.	Position of Sun and Moon at New Moon
	Sun	Moon		
Bentley	349° 10' 08"	355° 28' 15"	11h 35' 31"A.M.	348° 39' 34"
Lahiri	348° 14' 44"	352° 12' 49"	4h 11' 11"P.M.	347 55' 29"
K. Sri	349° 31' 01"	351° 6' 11"	12h 14' 24" Midday	349° 23' 24"

(E) Ending moment of New Moon and the then position of the sun and moon on the following important days—

Date	Week days from Sunday Sunrise	Position of the Sun and the Moon.	Remarks
17 Feb. 3102 B.C.	Th. 4.26	349°.39	
10 Jan. 3104 B.C.	Sat. 6.46	312°.61	26 lunations earlier = 767.80 days = 756°.78
11 Dec. 3105 B.C.	Th. 4.93	283°.52	1 lunation earlier = 29.53 days = 29°.09
23 Dec. 3106 B.C.	Sun. 0.57	294°.25	12 lunations earlier = 354.37 days = 349°.27

Special Note :

Sat. 13 Dec. 3105 B. C. and Sunday 11 Jan. 3104 B. C. are both Sukla Prathama Thithi with the Sun and Moon at 283°.52 and 312°.611. A number of friends pointed out that 11 Jan. 3104 B. C. is the Real Magha Sukla Prathama. I thank them for their suggestion. Hence Vyasa's Astronomical *Kali Yuga began on Sunday 11 Jan. 3104 B.C.*

F. Position of the Planets at midnight Th/Fri, 17/18 Feb 3102 B C at Kurukshatra.

Planet	Mean position according to Bentley — Lahiri		Correct apparent position — K. Sri
Mer	315°58'30"	314°58'37"	335°33
Venus	22° 0'55"	21°19'25"	20°47'
Mars	337°42'30"	336°37'30"	345°37'
Jupiter	5°38'32"	5°14'21"	3°43'
Saturn	329° 0'43"	328°58'50"	324°36'
Rahu	194° 2' 0"	193°54'50"	189°40'

According to Bentley and Lahiri, Mercury is about 35° from the Sun. This is not astronomically correct. This mistake is due to taking mean positions, which usually give very erroneous conclusions. The same is true of Venus and the other planets

G. Correct apparent position of the planets on the midnight of Sat/Sun, 10/11 Jan. 3104 B.C.

Mercury	298° 58'
Venus	298° 16'
Mars	299° 25'
Jupiter	299° 10'
Saturn	299° 5'
Rahu	230° 22'

i.e. at 5 A. M. on the 10th Jan. 3104 B.C. the planets were seen rising clustered together at Mid Srawishta, with the crescent Moon. (The difference in longitude between the planets and the sun is about 15° or one hour). Hence *Sunday, 11th Jan 3104 B. C. the Magha Sukla* Prathama of Veda Vyasa is *the beginning of the astronomical Kali Yuga Era.*

H.   *Detailed method of the calculation of the positions of Rahu and the planets.*

I. Rahu

(i) Position of Rahu on 1st Kaliday i.e. at midnight of Th/Fri, 17/18 Feb. 3102 B. C.

(a) No. of Kalidays to 1st Jan. 1968 = 1851391 and position of Rahu on 1st Jan. 1968 = 0° 35′10″ ∴ position of Rahu on 1st Kaliday.

$$= \frac{1851391}{6793.\overline{4664}} \times 360° + 0° \ 35′ \ 10″$$

$$= 189° \ 4′ \ 59″ + 0° 35′ \ 10″$$

(b) $= 189° \ 40′ \ 09″ = \underline{189° \ 40′}$

Aliter : Re—Perpetual Ephemeris—Epoch position of Rahu on 1809755 Kaliday = 47°0′39″ Motion in 1809755 days

$$= 360° \times \frac{1809755}{6793.47} = 142° \ 39′11″ \ \therefore \text{Position on Kaliday}$$

1st $= 189° 39′50″ = 189°40′$

(ii) Position of Rahu on—768 Kaliday at midnight on Sunday 11th Jan 3104 B. C.

Motion for 768 days $= 40° \ 41′ \ 53″$

∴ Position $= 189° \ 40′ \ 09″ + 40° \ 41′ \ 53″$

$$= 230° 22′02″ = \underline{230° 22′}$$

II Saturn

b (i) Position of Saturn on 1st Kali day at midnight 17/18 Feb. 3102 B.C.

169 sidereal periods of Saturn = 1818308.149073 days

4978 .... Sun = 1818248.838244 ,,

Difference = 59.310829 days

i.e. Saturn is behind the sun by $\dfrac{59.310839}{10759.219817} \times 360°$

= 1° 58'59"

Key date for Perpetual Ephemeris = 1811248.84th Kaliday = Wednesday, 4th April 1877 A.D.

Position of Saturn that day = 322° 36' 58"

∴ Position on 1st Kali day = 322° 36' 58" + 1° 58, 59" = 324° 36'

b (ii) Position of Saturn at midnight on-768 Kali day i.e. Sunday 11th Jan 3104 B.C.

Key date = 1818249 − 768 = 1817481 Kali day = Friday 26th Feb. 1875 A.D.

Position of Saturn on that day = 297° 5' 30"

Hance..... ....11th Jan 3104 B.C.
= 297°5'30" + 1°58'58"
= 299°5'

III Jupiter

c (i) Position of jupiter on the midnight of 17/19 Feb. 3102 B.C.

420 sidereal periods of jupiter = 1824017. 6248 days

4964........................sun = 1824092.9507 ,,

Difference = 75.3259 days

i.e. Jupiter is in advance of the sun

by $\dfrac{75.3259}{4332.58482} \times 360° = \underline{6° \ 15' \ 32''}$

Key date = 1824093 Kali day = Tuesday, 4th April 1893 A.D. Position of Jupiter that day = 9° 58' 15''

∴ Position of Jupiter on 18 Feb 3102 B.C. = 9° 58' 15''−6° 15'32'' = 3 42' 43'' = $\underline{3° \ 43'}$

c (ii) Position of Jupiter on–768 Kali day i.e. 11 Jan 3104BC

Key date = 1824093 − 768 = 1823325 Kali day
= Thursday 26th Feb 1891 A.D.

Position of Jupiter on that day = 305° 25' 26''

i.e.........11 Jan 3104 BC=305° 25' 26'' − 6° 15' 32''
= 299° 09' 54'' = 299° 10'

IV Mars

d (i) Position of Mars on 18 Feb. 3102 B.C.

2643 sidereal periods of Mars = 1815687.201735 days

4971 .... Sun = 1815691.5528   ,,

Difference = 4.3311 days

i.e. Mars is in advance of Sun by 4.3311 days

$= \dfrac{4.3311}{686.979645} \times 360° = 2° \ 16'$

Key date = 1815691.55 Kali day = Monday 4th April 1870 A.D.

Position of Mars that day = 347° 53'

∴ ......on 18 Feb 3102 B.C.
= 347°53' − 2°16' = $\underline{345° \ 37'}$

d (ii) Position of Mars on 11 Jan 3104 B.C.

Key date = 1815691.55 − 768 = 1814923.55 Kali day
= Wednesday, 26th Feb. 1868 A.D.

Position of Mars on that day = 302° 41'

∴ ......11th Jan 3104 B.C. = 302° 41' − 2°16'

= 300° 25' − 1° for correction = 299° 25'

V Venus

c (i) Position of Venus on 18 Feb. 3102 B.C.

8061 sidereal periods of Venus = 1811321.096946days

4959...........................Sun = 1811308.957082 „

Difference = 12.1398 days

i.e. Venus is behind the sun by $\dfrac{12.1398}{224.701786} \times 360°$

= 19° 27'

Key date = 1811309 Kali day = Sunday, 4th April 1858 A.D.

Position of Venus on that day = 1° 20' 6"

∴ ....18 Feb 3102 B.C. = 1° 20' 6" + 19° 27'

= 20° 47'

(ii) Position of Venus on 11 Jan 3104 B.C.

Key date = 1811309 − 768 = 1810541 Kali day
= Tuesday, 26th Feb. 1856 A.D.

Position of Venus on that day = 278° 49' 7"

∴ .... 11th Jan 3104 B.C. = 278° 49' + 19° 27'

= 298° 16'

VI Mercury

g (i) Position of Mercury on 18 Feb 3102 B.C.

20628 sidereal periods of Mercury = 1814595.8586days

4968........................... Sun = 1814596.2712512 days

Dif = .41256 days

i.e. Mercury is ahead of the sun by 1° 35'

Key date = 1814596.26 Kali day Friday 5th April 1867 A.D.

Position of Mercury that day $= 337° 7' 33"$

∴.............18 Feb. 3102 B.C. $= 337° 7' 33" - 1° 35'$

$= 335° 33'$

g (ii) Position of Mercury on 11th Jan. 3104 B.C.

Key Date $= 1814596.27 - 768 = 1813828.27$ Kali day

i.e. Tuesday 26th Feb. 1865 A.D.

Position of Mercury that day $= 300° 33' 25"$

∴.............11th Jan .3104 B.C. $= 300° 33' 25" - 1° 35'$

$= 298° 58'$.

These results have been verified with "the Indian Ephemeris" method of Dewan Bahadur Swami Kannu Pillai·

———

Conclusion

I thank all those friends who wrote their congratulations, opinions, and suggestions regarding my work. I hope this appendix will satisfy everyone of them, since it answers all the problems raised by them. I request the readers to go through the calculations and write to me if there are any further points to be clarified.

I The Kali Era (of the Vedanga Jyotisha Saptha Rishi Era) began with the 5476th year of the S.R. Era, on the Magha Sukla Prathama day of the year "Samvatsara" on Sunday (0.75) 23rd Dee 3106 B.C. with the Sun and Moon at 284.25 of the present Indian Zodiac. The two worked examples prove the correctness of the above result. Similar problens may be worked for the Magha Sukla Prathama of any Indian year.

II. The Ritualistic Kali Yuga began on 13th Oct. 3105 B.C. at the beginning of Sarad Ruthu and Margasira month, with the Sun and Moon at Jyeshta Nakshatra (226°) on the early morning of Tuesday, true to the old saying, (Kettai, Mootai Sevvai kizhamai) Jyeshta, Amavasya, coupled with the early morning of Tuesday. The tradition is that their combination forebodes an evil epoch.

III. It was on the next Magha Sukla Prathama, Sunday, 11th Jan 3104 BC, that the Astronomical Kali Era began. It was then, with the New Moon ending on Saturday (6.46) with the sun and Moon at 312.61 of the Zodiac, all the planets were together at 299°. For a day or two earlier, at about 5 A.M. all the planets were seen clustered together, with the crescent Moon. Hence the statement that at Kali Era beginning the planets were together at (Midshravishta) the Zero point of the then Zodiac.

Thus was Kali Yuga ushered in.

Extracts from a few letters

1. Your approach seems to be in the right direction, and perhaps you may be able to help in clarifying our ideas about our eras, epochs and chronology.

— Sri D. R. Mankad, Prof. of Chronology and Vice-Chanceller, Sowrashtra University.

2. I must congratulate you on your brilliant exposition about traces of the first civilisation on this planet.

— Sri Vaidya Guru Dutt, M.M.SC., (New Delhi)

3. The equation with Sravishta is most brilliant. It should become an accepted date for the beginning of Kali Era. It has removed many hurdles of our ancient history. Your reasoning of Kali beginning is convincing.

— Sri Bhagavad Datta, M.A. New Delhi.

4. On reading your thesis I find it of vital and fundamental importance to a study of Indian and world history.

— Sri P. N. Oak, M.A., L.L.B., President of the Institute for re-writing Indian History.

5. I congratulate you for your marvellous finding which will surely be a turning point in the history of Indian Chronology.

— Sri Radha Shyam Shastri, B.A., L.L.B., Haryana.

6. The paper is very illuminating and is likely to throw much light on the selection of the Kali Epoch.

— Sri N. C. Lahiri, M.A. Secretary, Calendar Reform Committee of the Govt. of India, Calcutta.

13

7. The Indian nation is indebted to you for your services in establishing that Kali Yugadhi and Maha Bharata are not myths, but real astronomical and chronological facts.

—Prof. V. Rajagopalan, M A., Professor of Sanskrit,
Vivekananda College, Madras.

8. You have correctly hit on the nail when you observe that "it was an unholy day the European orientalists introduced the word Aryan race..." I have expressed this forcibly in my articles and lectures..."

—Dr. B. V. Raman, M. Litt., Editor,
Astrological Magazine, Bangalore.

———

1. Article on "Kali Yugadhi"—was published in the Bhavan's Journal Vol. XIV No. 6 Oct. 1967

2. Article on "Kali Yugadhi"—was published in the Bulletin of the Institute of Traditional cultures, Madras University 1968

3. Article on "Cradle of Man" was published in the Journal of the Indian Geographical Society, Special Number-re-International Geographical Congress held at Delhi in Dec. 1968